ELLIOT FRY'S
GOOD·BYE

BY LARRY DANE BRIMNER
PICTURES BY EUGENIE FERNANDES

BOYDS MILLS PRESS

Text copyright © 1994 by Larry Dane Brimner
Illustrations copyright © 1994 by Eugenie Fernandes

Published by Caroline House
Boyds Mills Press, Inc.
A Highlights Company
815 Church Street
Honesdale, Pennsylvania 18431
Printed in Mexico

Publisher Cataloging-in-Publication Data
Brimner, Larry Dane.
    Elliot Fry's good-bye / by Larry Dane Brimner ; pictures
by Eugenie Fernandes.—1st ed.
[32]p. : col. ill. ; cm.
Summary : Young Elliot leaves home when he learns he must share
his room with his uncle.
ISBN 1-56397-113-5
[1. Family life—Fiction.] I. Fernandes, Eugenie, ill. II. Title.
[E]—dc20   1994
Library of Congress Catalog Card Number 92-73993

First edition, 1994
Book designed by Leslie Bauman
The text of this book is set in 16-point Hiroshige Book.
The illustrations are done in gouache and watercolors.
Distributed by St. Martin's Press

10 9 8 7 6 5 4 3 2 1

#29613958

Elliot Fry left home one bright, sunny, perfectly fine day.

Until then he had liked his home. Sure, his mom reminded him now and then not to track mud on her shiny kitchen floor.

"It wasn't me," Elliot tried to explain. "It was my boots."

His mom wouldn't have it. "OUT," she said, waving a mop in the general direction of the yard.

His dad sometimes complained that he made too much noise.

"Okay," Elliot said, putting down his hammer and picking up his harmonica. "I'll make music."

But his dad wasn't happy about that either. "NOT NOW, Elliot!" he said, clapping his hands over his ears. "I'm trying to think."

And his sister, Sara, tattled on everybody, but usually it was on Elliot.

"MOM!" Sara cried out. "Elliot's bouncing on my bed again."

It wasn't easy, but he could live with all that. Then on that bright, sunny, perfectly fine day his mom said, "Elliot, help me straighten your room so Uncle Abe will have a place to stay."

"Why can't Uncle Abe stay in somebody else's room?" asked Elliot.

"Your room has bunk beds," his mom said. "Somewhere."

"But this is *my* room," complained Elliot. "It's not fair! I'M LEAVING!"

"Fine," his mom said. "You may borrow your dad's suitcase."

And that's exactly what he did. He lugged his dad's suitcase upstairs and packed Spout, his elephant, inside it.

"You might need some clothes," his dad mentioned. "It could get cold where you're going."

"I thought about that," Elliot said (even though he hadn't really thought about it at all).

"You'd better take a snack," his mom suggested. "It might take a long time to get to where you're going."

"I planned to do that," Elliot said (even though he hadn't really planned that at all).

"I'm leaving," Elliot said later, thump-thump-thumping the suitcase down the stairs.

"I'm leaving NOW," Elliot said as he opened the front door.

"I'M LEAVING RIGHT THIS VERY SECOND!" Elliot shouted, tugging his wagon up the walk.

"Have a good trip, dear," his mom said.

"Good-bye," he said weakly and wondered what went wrong.

When he reached Mr. Nelson's house next door, Elliot's mom hollered, "Elliot?" Elliot looked back. "Did you pack a sweater?"

Elliot sighed. "Yes," he said, continuing on his way. He passed the Witts' house, the Garcias' house, and the Cottons' house.

"Elliot?" his dad called when Elliot got to Mrs. Gregg's house at the corner. "Don't forget you're not allowed to cross the street."

"I won't," said Elliot as he stomped around the corner. There. He had left!

On his second trip around the block, Elliot decided he was hungry. "This looks like a good place to have a snack," he said. He had a potato-chip-and-dill-pickle sandwich under Mr. Nelson's tree, and nobody once said "OUT."

On his third trip around the block, he noticed the hammock Mr. Nelson liked so much. "What a great swing!" he yelped. He swung and hooted, and nobody once said "NOT NOW, Elliot" or "I'm trying to think."

In fact nobody said anything at all to Elliot Fry. Not
even when it began to turn cool. So Elliot wrapped
himself up in his sweater and held Spout by his side.
He began to think it might be nice to hear somebody
call his name. Then Elliot heard laughter.

"I wonder what's so funny," he said to Spout.
"Let's go see."

He stood on his porch and peeked in the window. Just then the screen door opened. "Elliot?"

"Uncle Abe!" Elliot said.

"I came all this way for a good, old-fashioned sleepover," said Uncle Abe, "but you had left."

"A sleepover?" Elliot asked.

"Mmmmm." Uncle Abe nodded. "I fixed popcorn, but there was no one to throw it at."

Elliot understood. Half the fun of sleepover popcorn was the fight.

"I told myself a scary story," Uncle Abe said, "but it wasn't as bloodcurdling as yours."

Elliot understood. No one could curdle blood better.

"I even brought my flashlight." Uncle Abe showed him. "But it's not the same."

Elliot understood. He knew just where to put his chin to make the best spooky face.

When it got dark, Elliot told the most bloodcurdling story ever—by flashlight.

"Ooooooo!" yelled Uncle Abe.

And when he did . . .

. . . the door flew open. The light clicked on.

"The three of us against the two of you," said Elliot's mom.

And Elliot's room was filled with a swirling blizzard of popcorn.